On a planet, f
away called Alcyone
lived a boy known as
Cosmos.
On this planet, lived
only a few thousand
people and this place
was full of nature.
Trees that stood as tall
as 1000 metres and
flowers that grew in
every colour, shape and
size one could imagine.
Everyone lived in
harmony and shared
their truth.

On this planet, people did not require words to speak with each other and they referred to this ability as telepathy. They could send their regards to people who lived in distant places, or let their family know about their safety by merely thinking about it.

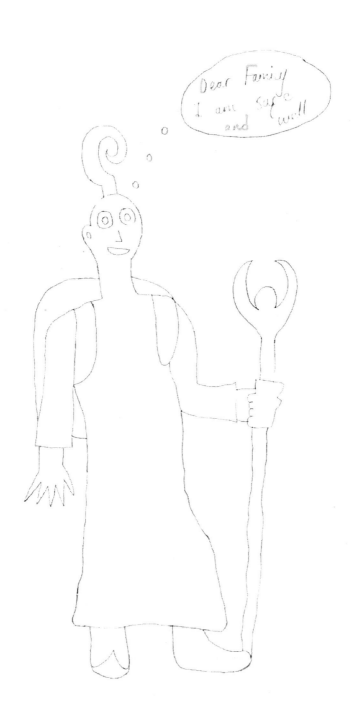

Everyone knew that connection was an integral part of the planet's survival. To show and give love was of great importance; through touch and thought.

Each month the oligarchic council would hold a ritual in which all the people celebrated the gift of life.

The ceremony consisted of four time frames.

The people would dance around the great fires, embrace the showers from the rain, swim in the lake of purity and rest on the foothills next to the illuminated forest.

Each night on this planet, the people would also pray to Gaia who was, in fact, a star known as the Dog Star. They called her Mother and paid her great respect every night.

Cosmos often wondered as he gazed at the stars, what it would be like to live on another planet.

As he grew older, he became part of the galactic federation and was sent on a research mission to planet earth.

He discovered that this planet was very different from his own.

People seemed distant from each other.

The concept of sharing on this planet was an unfamiliar one.

.

Some people would
take things that did not
belong to them from
other people

He noticed the anger and guilt that he had read of in the ancient libraries in Alcyone, existed on this planet and that it created some kind of instability or disharmony within the planet.
He learnt that people on this planet seemed to be afraid of love and afraid to express who they really were.

This created conflict.
He noticed some
people were
pretending to be
somebody they were
not, to fit in with
others.
This was all new to
Cosmos and as much
as it sparked his
interest, it also scared
him.
After all, how could he
ever trust the people
whose foundation was
built on everything
but love?

Being good at heart, Cosmos couldn't help wonder if there was a way he could magically blow a wave of love in the hearts of the humans that were burdened with hate and misery.
And if there was one thing Cosmos mastered in, it was the art of thinking.
Cosmos came up with an idea.

Cosmos was living in the woods adjacent to a town called Everdeen. It was away from the human eye. There was a man he saw going to work at 8am every day. Cosmos decided to telepathically communicate with him. Cosmos also decided to start slowly with his idea so he did not overwhelm humanity with a sudden

tsunami of compassion.
The man was known as
Jack and Cosmos
waited until he came
home and had gone to
bed.
Through his dream,
Cosmos showed Jack a
world full of
unhappiness where
people felt lonely and
in need of love and
care.
Cosmos further
showed him humans
had a lack of empathy
for others and how
they surrounded
themselves

in their own bubble as
far as their personal
needs were concerned.

After Cosmos had showed Jack this dream for a whole week, he failed to witness any changes in his behaviour. One day, Cosmos was sat camouflaged in a tree and as usual he watched as Jack came out of his home to leave for work. Surprisingly, Jack greeted the first person who he saw instead of just walking past. Jack also greeted a man who had set up his stall in front of the sidewalk. Cosmos smiled to himself and even though it wasn't much, he thought it was better than nothing.

Days went by.
And one morning Jack noticed an old lady whose wheelbarrow's wheel had got stuck in a ditch.
Without giving it much thought, Jack reached out and began helping the old lady.
Jack's behaviour was improving in a way that he actually began noticing his surroundings instead of just going about his day in his own world.

He had started to lend a helping hand to those in need.

One day, not far from his home, a car had broken down in the middle of the road. Jack moved forward and began helping the man to push the vehicle in order to try and get it started again. After a while, inspired by Jack, several more people came and began pushing the car.

Slowly, Jack's habits started getting noticed by more and more people. He began to infuence others and it inspired something within them to do better as well. Within days, the entire town transformed into a little hub where everyone knew everyone and the flowers of love were blooming everywhere.

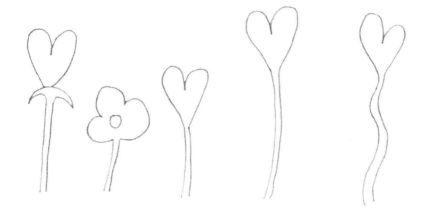

Love and joy flowed
through the people's
hearts and soon they
realized that the way to get
love was to give it.

The newfound treasure of compassion and empathy gave birth to melodic frequencies in the air that reflected the alluring beauty of the flowers.

Cosmos felt more at peace for bringing a change on planet Earth far more than he cared about the research mission he had originally come for.
His work on this planet was done and he was hopeful for a future where everyday someone was positively impacted by the benevolence of the town of Everdeen.

Printed in Poland
by Amazon Fulfillment
Poland Sp. z o.o., Wrocław

89713602R00020